Walks with Augustus

PRAISE FOR *STORYSHARES*

"One of the brightest innovators and game-changers in the education industry."
– Forbes

"Your success in applying research-validated practices to promote literacy serves as a valuable model for other organizations seeking to create evidence-based literacy programs."

- Library of Congress

"We need powerful social and educational innovation, and Storyshares is breaking new ground. The organization addresses critical problems facing our students and teachers. I am excited about the strategies it brings to the collective work of making sure every student has an equal chance in life."
– Teach For America

"Around the world, this is one of the up-and-coming trailblazers changing the landscape of literacy and education."
- International Literacy Association

"It's the perfect idea. There's really nothing like this. I mean wow, this will be a wonderful experience for young people."   - Andrea Davis Pinkney, Executive Director, Scholastic

"Reading for meaning opens opportunities for a lifetime of learning. Providing emerging readers with engaging texts that are designed to offer both challenges and support for each individual will improve their lives for years to come. Storyshares is a wonderful start."
- David Rose, Co-founder of CAST & UDL

Walks with Augustus

L.V. Halo

STORYSHARES

Story Share, Inc.
New York. Boston. Philadelphia

Published in the United States by Story Share, Inc.

Storyshares
Story Share, Inc.
24 N. Bryn Mawr Avenue #340
Bryn Mawr, PA 19010-3304
www.storyshares.org

Inspiring reading with a new kind of book.

Interest Level: High School
Grade Level Equivalent: 2.7

9781973487500

Book design by Storyshares

Printed in the United States of America

Storyshares Presents

1

I stood in front of the brick row house and grumbled. I was alone on the sidewalk. There was no one to hear my complaining, but I did it anyway. I thought maybe grumbling would make me feel better. It didn't. I pushed my long black hair out of my eyes. I stared up at the building.

This was Grandma Lollie's place. Lollie wasn't actually my grandmother. I don't think she was anyone's grandmother, really. But everyone called her that.

Lollie lived in a quiet part of Jersey City. It was a ten minute bus ride from my house up the hill and not too long a walk from Morse High, my new school. I had just started there as a freshman in September.

The cold November wind blew hard and pushed me sideways. I regretted the holes I'd cut into my new black jeans. My mom had been pretty mad at me for cutting into the new fabric. I was beginning to agree with her.

Another gust of wind hit me. My choices were to either freeze on the sidewalk, or venture inside Grandma Lollie's building. I hadn't been inside her apartment since I was a kid.

I liked Grandma Lollie. She was always walking around the city with her red shopping cart, her little white dog, and her big smile. But I was dreading seeing her. She was sick, and I wasn't sure what to expect.

I slowly made my way up the cement steps, thinking of the conversation I'd had with my mom during dinner the night before.

We'd just finished our salad when she said, "I got a call today. Grandma Lollie's had a stroke."

She'd spooned some mac and cheese into my bowl. My mom always made mac and cheese from a box and still always managed to mess it up. It kind of glopped off the spoon into the bowl. Gross.

"That's sad," I'd replied. Truthfully, I was thinking more about the mac and cheese than Grandma Lollie. I'd tasted it. It was clumpy and gluey. Not a good combination.

"It is. She's been a pillar of the community for decades."

My mom always spoke like that. She worked for an environmental group, so she was used to talking to politicians. So she called Grandma Lollie a "pillar of the community" instead of just saying that everybody knew her.

I'd made a move to turn on the TV. My mom had cleared her throat. I'd put down the remote and turned back to face her.

"I got another call today, too. From your school," she'd said. I'd winced. I knew that was coming. "You failed two of your midterms," she'd said. "What happened?"

I stabbed at some macaroni with my fork. "I don't know," I'd said. Actually, I did know. I'd tried to study, I really did. But history was epically boring. I had to physically hold my eyes open while I read the textbook. Even when I did that, it seemed like the words flew right out of my head the second my eyes passed over them. I couldn't remember anything. And algebra... well, that kind of went without saying. I had no clue what I was doing in that class.

"Well, you'd better figure it out. It's unacceptable," she'd said. "I know you've had a hard time since dad and I split up. But it's time to get your act together."

"I'll do better! Geez," I'd said. My voice was shrill and whiney. I hated it when I sounded that way, but sometimes I couldn't help it. Especially with my mom. She expected me to be just like her. School had come easily to her.

"You're in high school now. There's no time for messing around. Is your homework even done for tomorrow?" she'd asked.

She'd had me there. I'd spent the afternoon hanging out in the pizza place with my best friends, Asha and Natalie. I'd been separated from them when my mom and I moved, and I was districted to Morse High.

"I'm doing it after dinner," I'd said.

"Sofia, that's unacceptable. When I was in high school my dad made me finish all my homework before anything else. TV, friends, whatever. I had no fun until the work was completed."

"So, what? I should just have, like, no social life at all? Great," I'd moaned.

"No, of course I want you to have friends. But the pizzeria isn't exactly the best place to do your algebra," my mom had said.

"So, am I grounded or something?" I'd asked.

"Not exactly," she'd begun. She took a bite of the mac and cheese. It was cold by then, and she'd made a face. Even if she didn't miss being married to my dad, I knew she missed his cooking.

"You know Grandma Lollie has that little dog. Well, the neighbor's tell me that she used to walk it several miles a day. Can you believe it? At almost 90 years old."

She took a sip of water. "Anyway, Lollie has a nurse to help take care of her. But the nurse doesn't take care of the dog."

I wasn't seeing what this had to do with me. "And?"

"And it's going crazy, all cooped up. She needs someone to walk it every day. That's where you come in," she'd said.

"Me?" I'd asked. I didn't really like dogs.

"Yes, you. I've arranged for you to walk the dog every day after school. Then you can stay at the apartment and finish your homework," she' said.

"Mom, that sounds so boring!" I'd cried. "Why are you doing this to me?"

"Sofia, this isn't a punishment. I think you will find it rewarding to help someone in need," she'd said. She finished her bowl of macaroni.

That's what brought me to Grandma Lollie's building on this windy day. I rang the buzzer. I hoped no one would answer.

2

I waited about ten seconds. I was about to leave when an older man in blue surgical scrubs came to the door.

"You're here for the dog?" he said gruffly.

"Y-yes," I stammered.

"Good, good. Come inside," he said, waving me in. He led me down the hall to Grandma Lollie's door.

He called out, "Grandma, the girl is here for Augustus!" It was funny to see this tough man call someone "grandma." There was no reply as I scooted through the door.

The apartment was neat and prim. There were lace doilies on the backs of all the chairs. The mantle had fancy looking figurines. Music played softly on an old record player. A hospital bed was near the front window. Grandma Lollie was in it, sitting up. Augustus, a scruffy white terrier, was curled up at her feet.

The nurse nudged me. "What's your name?"

"Sofia."

"Nice to meet you. I'm Mikhail." I realized that his accent was Russian. He turned back to Grandma Lollie. "Grandma, Sofia is here to walk Augustus. What does she need to know?"

I waited for her to speak. But instead she picked up a bunch of laminated sheets of paper with pictures on them. She began pointing at different pictures. Mikhail watched and nodded. I couldn't understand why she wasn't speaking.

When Lollie finished pointing at the pictures, Mikhail turned to me. "She wants you to walk Augustus for 45 minutes. Walk quickly so he can get some energy out. I'll get you his leash."

I must have looked confused. "She lost her speech when she had the stroke," Mikhail explained. "She's still feeling weak on her right side, but we'll get her good as new in no time." He smiled at Grandma Lollie.

I approached the bed. Grandma Lollie looked just like I remembered. Same ocean blue eyes. Same shoulder length blonde hair. Except now there was a little strip of white at the top of her head. I realized that this must be her real hair. I had somehow always thought her hair was still blond, even though she was almost 90.

I reached for the scraggly white dog. He growled. I jumped back.

Grandma Lollie smiled. She patted him and then nudged him toward me. He hopped down off the bed using a series of boxes laid out like stairs. He grumbled the whole time. Sort of like how I had been grumbling outside a few minutes ago.

Mikhail put Augustus's leash on and handed him to me. "All yours, kid." When he said "kid," it sounded like "keed."

I took the leather gloves Mikhail offered me and headed out. Augustus dragged behind me. He kept glancing back at Grandma Lollie. His nails made a scraping sound along the wood floor. Mikhail motioned for me to keep going. When we made it out to the hallway, Mikhail closed the door behind us.

3

I looked down at the little dog. "Let's go for a walk," I said. I tried to sound enthusiastic. His ears perked up for a second. But then he turned back to the door and scratched. He didn't want to walk with me any more than I wanted to walk with him. Somehow, I didn't think my mom would accept this excuse.

I bent down and tried to pick him up. As soon as my hands were around his belly, Augustus let out a low growl. I let him go. "Okay, okay, you crazy dog," I said.

Just then I heard a deep laugh and I jumped. I hadn't realized that the dumb dog was making me so nervous.

"Sorry to scare you," a voice said. I turned and saw someone hobbling down the stairs. The boy looked a little older than me.

He was tall, with close-cropped black hair and amber colored skin. I felt like I had seen him before. When he arrived at the bottom of the stairs, he reached down to Augustus with something in his hand. The dog snatched it and started chewing furiously.

"Slim Jims," the mysterious boy said, flashing his green eyes at me. It made my stomach flutter. "Augustus loves Slim Jims," he said. "That's the only way to get him to do anything." He scratched behind the dog's ears. "I'm Omar, by the way. I live upstairs."

"I'm Sofia. I'm supposed to be walking Augustus for Grandma Lollie." I was embarrassed to say such a babyish name in front of this guy.

"I figured. Yeah, keep some snacks in your pocket and he'll follow you." He held out a baggie of cut up Slim Jims. I put them in my pocket.

"Thanks," I said. "But he doesn't seem to like me."

Omar laughed again. "He doesn't like anyone much. Took two years before he stopped growling at me. Two years and tons of treats. Now we're buddies."

"Then why don't *you* walk him?" I asked.

He pointed to the cast on his leg. "Leg's busted. From football. I might need surgery."

"Oh, sorry," I said.

"Hey, don't you go to Morse?" he asked.

I nodded.

"Me too," he said. A voice called to him from upstairs. "Anyway, I gotta go. Good luck with Augustus," he said.

"Thanks," I said quietly. I watched him as he slowly and painstakingly made his way back upstairs.

4

I could still smell the Slim Jims on Augustus's breath as we hopped down the cement steps and onto the slate sidewalk. Slim Jims. They had a special place in my heart. They were my dad's favorite snack. Even though my dad was a chef, he always loved them. They were the only junk food he ever ate. When he packed his bag for Vegas, I hid a stash of them in his carry-on.

He had texted me from the airport: "Going to stink up the whole plane with my beef jerky smell. They have jerky in Vegas... it's not SO far. We'll see each other soon."

My parents broke up last summer. Then Dad got a job with a celebrity chef who was opening a new restaurant on the Vegas strip.

I was supposed to spend school breaks with him in Vegas.

He said he'd find a way for me to apprentice with the restaurants pastry chef. I thought about being in Vegas - hot air, swimming pools, the fast-paced thrill of the kitchen. A big contrast to trudging down the windy Jersey City street with a scruffy, ornery little dog.

At least Augustus seemed eager to walk. He trotted the streets with quick, efficient steps. Things were going pretty smoothly until we suddenly came face to face with a red haired lady and her pack of tiny poodles. The yappy little dogs surrounded us. Augustus started barking a high-pitched bark. He snapped at the fluffy poodles.

The lady yanked her dogs away from us. "Watch your dog!" she shouted at me as she walked off towards the park.

I didn't have time to respond. A cross-country team from Morse was jogging towards us from across the street. That set Augustus barking all over again. I managed to drag him out of the way of the runners.

Letting Augustus bite the athletes probably wouldn't make me very popular at my new school.

Then the sidewalk was quiet again. Augustus began walking as if nothing had happened.

I didn't get this dog. If the sidewalk was empty, we were fine. But if other dogs, or people, or squirrels, or birds, or any other living thing at all passed by, then we had trouble. Augustus would yank forward on the leash, bark like crazy, and wag his tail. I started paying closer attention to our surroundings. I crossed the street if I saw a dog coming in the distance. Augustus seemed happy when the sidewalk was clear and we were going at good pace.

I, on the other hand, was miserable. My legs were getting numb in my ripped jeans and the holes in my old Converse sneakers let in the cold air. If the season continued on like this, I'd need a whole new wardrobe - one fit for an arctic explorer. I walked Augustus aimlessly. I should have planned a route before we started. When the 45 minutes were up, we were far away from Grandma Lollie's. We hurried back, our heads pressing into the wind. My teeth chattered, but Augustus just kept pushing forward.

It was about five o'clock by the time we got back to the brick row house. The sky had that bluish tint that meant it was getting dark. That was what I hated the most about winter. The early darkness was like a shadow cast on the whole world.

I texted my dad while I waited for Augustus to pee on one last tree stump. "Freezing my butt off in NJ," I wrote. "What's the temperature there?"

A few seconds later he texted back a picture of a palm tree outside the restaurant. "You don't wanna know! ;) Looking 4ward to Thanksgiving!" He was coming back for the holiday in a couple of weeks.

Augustus rubbed against my legs, and nipped at my glove. "Okay, okay," I said, and we climbed the stairs to the apartment.

5

Once we were inside the building, I let Augustus off the leash. He trotted smartly to the apartment door. He scratched at the door once and deliberately. Mikhail opened it and let him in. He poked his head out the door."Coming, Sofia? Your mother said you'd be staying to do homework."

Great. I was hoping to get out of that part.

I followed Augustus into the apartment. He got a drink of water and then hopped up on his makeshift cardboard box stairs to Grandma Lollie's bed. I grabbed my school bag and headed to the kitchen table.

Mikhail was preparing dinner, which was a casserole that someone had dropped off. The neighborhood was like that. Anytime something bad happened, people tried to cure it with food.

In my house, my dad used to make the "Get Well Soon" casseroles. After he moved out, my mom tried making one. She used tuna fish, a can of soup, and noodles. The smell was so awful I made her stop.

I plodded through my homework. Mikhail tidied the apartment, organized Grandma Lollie's bills, and checked on the casserole. He wasn't still for a minute. Even when he sat down for a cup of coffee, his hands were busy sorting her pills into a giant organizer.

Mikhail was a stocky, older man. His belly pressed tight against his sky blue scrub shirt. You wouldn't call him "elegant" when you first looked at him. But somehow he moved around the apartment as if he were a ballet dancer. There was never a wasted movement.

I turned back to my Spanish worksheet.

The other kids in my class looked at me funny when they heard my name on the first day.

"Sofia Alvarez?" the teacher called.

"Here," I mumbled. I heard the whispers and giggles from the other kids. I got it. What was a Hispanic kid doing in Spanish 1? Shouldn't I already speak Spanish, like, fluently?

But I didn't. I guess it would have been less embarrassing to just sign up for French or something. But I wanted to learn. I wanted to show my dad that I could speak Spanish when he visited.

I was a slow learner, though. The list of things I could say was pathetically short. I could say, "My name is Sofia and I am from Jersey City," and that was about it. The rest was just long lists of vocabulary words that I couldn't put together into sentences.

I finished up the rest of my homework, leaving the algebra for when I was home and my mom could help me. I packed up everything, put on my coat, and headed to the door.

"See you tomorrow," called Mikhail. Grandma Lollie waved. Augustus snored.

6

When I got home, I was tired and stiff from the cold. I tore my closet apart looking for the warmest clothes I had. Well, warmest and least dorky. An image of Omar flashed in my mind. He was really cute, but he was a football player. I was pretty sure he wouldn't be interested in me. For one thing, I was a freshman. Also, I was kind of weird and didn't have many friends at school.

Most of my shirts were thin black cotton. I figured I could layer them. I found some leggings I could wear under my black jeans. I left everything in a pile on my bedroom floor.

I spent the rest of my time until my mom got home listening to The Smiths, watching a cake decorating show, and painting my nails. It was Thursday - pizza night. For some reason, my mom and I always got along better when the food on the table was tasty.

My mom came home with the pizza, a couple of sodas, and a bag from Target. Before we dug into the pepperoni pie, she proudly showed me what was inside the red and white plastic bag.

She pulled things out one by one and announced them. "Long underwear. Scarf. Hat. Mittens." Brick red long underwear, pink scarf, orange mittens, and a blue hat. The items laid out on the table looked like a rainbow. Was she kidding?

"Mom, have you ever seen me in orange?" I cried. "What is all this stuff?"

"I heard the forecast on the way home. It's supposed to be even colder next week. I thought you'd appreciate having this stuff," she said. She seemed hurt, but I was mad.

"I would appreciate it if you didn't buy such insane looking things!" I said.

"So you don't want any of it?" she asked. Her eyes narrowed and she glared at me until I answered.

"I guess I'll take the long underwear," I said, shoving the hat, mittens, and scarf back in the bag. "You should take the other stuff back."

"Okay, Your Highness," she answered sarcastically.

I flipped on the TV and we ate dinner in stubborn silence. So much for the peace-making power of pepperoni.

7

My mom was still annoyed at me the next morning, and I didn't do anything to make it better. I felt kind of bad. I knew I should have thanked her for trying, but it felt like she didn't know me at all. Like she didn't even see me. I wore black all the time. I hadn't worn orange, and definitely not pink, in years.

She couldn't understand that I wasn't like her. School didn't come easily to me. Making friends didn't come easily, either.

Because of our fight, I hadn't asked her for help with my algebra homework. I tried to do it myself, but the mix of numbers and letters all over the worksheet confused me. I scratched in some guess answers and went to bed.

During fourth period math, I regretted that decision.

"Pop quiz!" my teacher, Ms. Warner, announced far too cheerfully.

I looked over the quiz. It was all related to the homework. The numbers swam together on the page. I couldn't focus. But I knew I couldn't fail another test! My mom would go crazy. If I had to retake math in summer school, I wouldn't get to go to Vegas for the summer. Maybe I wouldn't even be allowed to go for spring break. I tried and tried to remember what to do. The seconds ticked by.

"Five minutes!" Ms. Warner called out. I realized I was sweating. I looked around the room. Other kids were handing in their quizzes. The girl next to me looked like she knew what she was doing. If I could just see how she solved one of the problems, I might be able to figure out the rest of them.

I flicked my eyes to her paper. Then I looked at my teacher. She was busy grading. I looked back at the girl's paper. I began copying one of her equations. I had almost the entire thing down. I glanced up at my teacher again. She was staring right at me. I looked down quickly. I could feel my face turn red. I scribbled in some random answers. I handed in my quiz without looking at her. I didn't speak for the entire rest of the class.

When the bell finally rang I tried to slip out with the rest of the kids.

"Sophia," I heard Ms. Warner call just as I was about to escape. I crept up to her desk quietly. "I'm sure you know that we have a zero-tolerance policy for cheating here," she began. Her voice was calm, but I could tell she was angry.

"Yes," I replied meekly.

"I will have to give you a zero on the quiz," she continued. "I'm still deciding if I'm going to tell the principal."

I nodded.

"However," she added, "I will definitely be calling your mother."

I felt like I got punched in the stomach. The only thing my mom hated more than failing? Cheating.

I went through the rest of the day in a daze.

8

When I got to Grandma Lollie's, Mikhail was by her bedside. He was holding a can of nutritional smoothie. He looked frustrated.

"You have to drink this, Grandma," he pleaded. Grandma Lollie shook her head firmly.

"Please," he said. "It's the only way to get better." He offered her the blue can again. She waved it away, and it spilled on the floor. "Grandma!" he cried as he ran to get a dishtowel to clean it up.

"What's wrong?" I asked.

"She just won't eat or drink anything," he said, sighing deeply.

I picked up the empty can and sniffed inside. "You want her to drink this stuff?" I said. "It smells like a cake made of chemicals."

"It's a vitamin shake," said Mikhail. "It's good for her."

"Let me see what I can do," I said. Mikhail looked surprised as I headed towards the kitchen. When I was little, my dad would make me a delicious drink called almond milk. He always told me how healthy it was. "It's full of protein. That's what you need to grow strong," he would always say. Maybe it would work for Lollie. I dug around in the cabinets. I found a big bag of almonds, cinnamon, vanilla extract, and a tough looking blender.

Making almond milk with my dad was one of my earliest memories. He didn't go to work until the afternoon, so the morning was our special time. We would always set the almonds to soak first thing in the morning. Then we would go to the park or play games. I was thinking of this as I filled one of Lollie's mixing bowls with almonds and warm water. I left them to soak while I walked Augustus.

The walk was easier today than it had been yesterday. I was dressed for the weather and felt much warmer. We walked on quiet streets where we ran into less people. Augustus still growled when I tried to get him to do something he didn't want to. I bribed him with Slim Jims. When we got back to the apartment, he trotted in sweetly and jumped up with Grandma Lollie.

Instead of starting my homework I checked on my almonds. The dry nuts had gotten nice and plump from soaking in the water. I threw them into the blender. I added fresh water, too, and turned on the machine. It made a pretty awful sound as it ground up the nuts. Once the water, nuts, and spices were mixed, it was time to sweeten it a bit. I liked to use dates, a Middle Eastern fruit.

Grandma Lollie didn't have any. Mikhail suggested I ask Omar's mom, Nadia. I was a little nervous going up the stairs. I tried to smooth my hair before I knocked.

A little girl in pigtails came to the door. Omar appeared a second later.

"I need some dates," I blurted out. Omar smiled slyly. I realized how awkward that sounded. "I mean the fruit," I added.

He invited me in. The girl in pigtails was his sister Leila. He introduced me to his mom, Nadia. She had the same flashing green eyes as Omar. Her black hair was tucked into a dark red headscarf. She liked my idea of almond milk for Lollie. She gave me a bowl of plump dates. I told her she could try some when I finished.

I hurried downstairs to finish the almond milk. I put the pitcher in the fridge. Then I started my homework. I completed my Spanish worksheet and a paragraph for English in just twenty minutes. Something about cooking made it easier for me to focus. I was taking out my algebra when there was a knock at the door. It was Omar, his mom, and Leila.

"We'd love to try some almond milk, if it's ready," Nadia said.

I poured out six small glasses, including one with a straw for Grandma Lollie. I was suddenly nervous.

What if it was terrible? I took a small sip without looking at anyone. I held my breath while they tasted it.

I heard Leila squeal. Did she hate it?

No! She was drinking more and more. "Delicious!" said Mikhail. "Very creamy," said Nadia with approval. Omar smiled.

Grandma Lollie toasted me from her bed. I smiled and looked down. I could see my algebra worksheet still on the table, unfinished.

9

The wind didn't feel nearly so cold when I left Grandma Lollie's. I felt proud. I made something really good. Maybe it would even help Grandma Lollie.

I was still in a good mood when I came home. I felt inspired to keep cooking. I put on some music and found my dad's recipe for chocolate chip cookies. The cookies were just coming out of the oven when my mom got home.

"The apartment smells heavenly!" she said. She was smiling and looked more relaxed than I'd seen her in a long time. She had another bag from Target. I looked at the bag cautiously. I didn't want to get in another fight about clothes. My mom grabbed a cookie off the cooling rack.

"I got a call on my way home from work," she said.

Suddenly my good mood disappeared. My teacher. The quiz. My cheeks flushed and felt hot. I braced myself.

"It was Grandma Lollie's nurse. What's his name?" she asked.

I breathed a sigh of relief. "Mikhail," I replied.

"That's right," she said between bites of cookie. "He told me that you made some delicious protein shake for Grandma Lollie."

I felt proud all over again, but tried to hide it. "It wasn't a big deal," I said.

"Well, it was a big hit. So much that he's put in an order. He wants to buy it from you every week."

"Cool!" I exclaimed. I didn't care about hiding my pride anymore.

That night, we ate cookies and milk for dinner. We watched movies, and laughed a lot. It was the happiest our apartment had seemed in a long time.

10

The next day was Saturday. When I woke up, my mom was out on her run. A folded pile of black knitted items sat on the kitchen table. There was a note from my mom on top:

Sofia,

Sorry I was grouchy about the other stuff. I hope you like these. But if you don't, that's okay, too.

Love,

Mom

I unfolded everything. There was a black scarf with silver sparkles. A black hat with a little silver skull on it. A thick, black pair of mittens. I couldn't believe it. She got it completely right.

Even though it was the weekend, I still had to walk Augustus.

It was nice outside, so I decided to go over early. I left a note for my mom and then I hopped on the bus.

When I got to Lollie's, Augustus was snoozing by her side. The sun was shining through the window and warming her bed. One of the neighbors had come by that morning to do her hair. It was golden blond again, no more white stripe. It was curled perfectly, too. Lollie looked the happiest I'd seen her since I started coming to walk the dog. Mikhail had put on one of Lollie's favorite Ella Fitzgerald records. She patted time on Augustus's rump.

Lollie gestured for me to come sit with her. I pulled up a chair to her bedside.

"Is it really awful not being able to talk?' I asked her. Then I regretted it.

She smiled, and shrugged a little.

She picked up a white board and marker from the folds of the blankets and began to write slowly.

"What's this?" I exclaimed. Lollie hadn't had enough strength to write before.

Mikhail walked over. "We've been working hard with the physical therapist, right Lollie?" he said, giving her shoulder a squeeze. "She has been doing the exercises over and over every day. She has made wonderful progress. Soon we'll hear her voice again," he said.

Lollie turned the white board around to show me what she had written. I had asked her if it was hard not to talk, and she wrote in wiggly letters, "It's good to listen, too."

11

Augustus and I walked out in the golden afternoon light. The sycamore trees that lined the sidewalk were shedding their bark as well as their leaves. Augustus grabbed a piece of bark and threw it in the air. He jumped and ran in circles. He kept tossing it and catching it. It was the first time I'd ever seen him play.

"Maybe you're not such a grouch after all, Augustus," I said. After a few minutes, I gave a gentle tug on the leash and off we went. The walk wasn't so bad. It was still boring, but I didn't hate every second of it.

When we got back to the apartment, Omar was sitting on the stoop. His leg with the cast was propped up on one of the steps. His crutches were leaning on the banister.

"Are you locked out or something?" I asked.

"Nah, just getting some fresh air. Hate being cooped up in there. I should be starting track by now."

"You play football *and* run track? Geez," I said. "No wonder you broke your leg."

"Ha ha," he said sarcastically. "Now help me up, I want to take a walk with you guys."

"With us?" I said, feeling nervous.

"Yeah, just take me around the block once. I'm pretty slow, but I really need the exercise," he said. He reached out his hand. I took it and helped him up. I was glad I was wearing mittens. At least he couldn't feel my hands starting to sweat. He hopped up and shifted his body onto his crutches. It was hard to look cool on crutches, but somehow he was doing it. He rocked along beside me. My own steps felt suddenly awkward.

"So, how do you like Morse High so far?" Omar asked.

Ugh. "It's pretty awful," I replied.

"Oh, come on, we're not so bad," he said, elbowing me gently.

"Yeah, you kind of are," I elbowed back. "Everyone is obsessed with sports and smells like Slim Jims."

Omar laughed. "Well, you got us there." He was quiet for a moment. "Really though, why don't you like it?"

All the reasons I always gave my mom popped into my head. I hated the teachers. The other kids thought I was weird.

The school actually did smell bad, too. Like old socks when you got near the gym.

But I didn't say any of these. I surprised myself with the answer I gave. "I don't know. I guess I was just planning on going to Kennedy with all my friends. This is new and uncomfortable. And maybe I just don't want to like it."

I worried that I'd said too much. But then Omar nodded. "That's probably the most honest answer I've ever heard."

I blushed. "What about you?" I said. "I guess you love it there."

"Eh, it's okay," he said. "The leg has been a real drag. And I'm not actually obsessed with sports. I just do one every season. I hope I get good enough at one to get a college scholarship."

"And are you good enough?" I asked.

"Maybe I would have been, for track. But probably not now."

"I'm sorry," I said, and meant it.

He shrugged. "Get the cast off next week, so we'll see then."

We rounded the corner and were back on Lollie's street. I held his crutches while he hopped up the stairs.

He turned back to me before heading up the stairs to his apartment.

"It's really cool what you're doing for Lollie. I can tell it makes her happy," he said.

"Thanks," I said.

"I hope you start to like Morse soon," he called over his shoulder.

Maybe now I had a reason to.

12

When I dropped off Augustus, he was tired and happy. I made the mistake of trying to pet him. He barked sharply at me and flashed his teeth. "Okay, Augustus," I laughed. "Maybe next time."

I had Sunday off because Lollie's niece was visiting. My mom was away at a rally in the state capital, so I had the day to myself. I texted Asha and Natalie. Finally we were able to meet at the pizza place. It felt like forever since I'd seen them.

We met at the pizzeria and sat in our usual booth. "Oh my gosh, where have you been?" Natalie squealed when she saw me. Asha gave me a big hug. We talked about everything I had missed. Asha was running for Student Council, and Natalie had a date for the Winter Dance.

"Except I can't find a dress!" Natalie said dramatically. Then she brightened up. "You have to come shopping with us! We're going to the mall on Tuesday after school."

I fidgeted. I did want to go. "I can't. I have to walk Augustus."

"Can't someone else do it one time?" Natalie begged.

"We need you!" Asha chimed in.

"Guys, I really can't. I'm sorry."

Natalie pouted for a few minutes, until some new topic excited her.

It felt good to see them, but also a little strange. They were making all kinds of new friends. They had a bunch of new inside jokes and stories about people I'd never heard of. And I hadn't told them about Omar. That felt strange too. Not that there was really anything to tell. But we used to share all our secrets.

It felt like something had changed.

13

The strange feeling stayed with me through to Monday. I was still thinking about my friends when I walked into 4th period math. Then I froze. The pop quiz. I'd actually forgotten about what happened last week. But, my teacher had never called my mom. Maybe she had forgotten, too? It was all I could hope.

I squirmed through the entire class, feeling nervous. I tried to make myself invisible. When class ended I tried to slip out the door. Ms. Warner called me up to her desk.

"Sofia, I wanted to let you know that I talked to your mom this morning."

Oh no. "Okay," I said.

"Your mom said this wasn't like you, and I believe her. Nothing like this happened at your other school. What's going on?"

I tried to explain that I wasn't exactly cheating, that I was just trying to jog my memory. She didn't look like she believed me.

"If you're having trouble with what we're learning, you should stay after school for extra help," she said.

"I can't!" I cried. "I have to walk Lollie's dog." I explained all about Lollie and her stroke and Augustus.

"I can tell you're a good kid. I'm not going to tell the principal, but this can't happen again," she said.

I nodded, but it wasn't really the principal I was worried about. Dealing with my mom would be way worse. The minutes in school ticked by. Each one brought me closer to being in major trouble. It would have been better if I had told my mom about the cheating myself. Now I would get in trouble for not just cheating, but lying, too.

Being nervous made me grouchy. When I arrived at Grandma Lollie's, Augustus didn't want to get off the bed. I tried to pull him off. He snapped at me. I pulled my hand away in time, but it bounced off of one of his teeth. It hurt. And it scared me. My eyes filled up with tears. I couldn't help it. I didn't want to cry. But once I started it was hard to stop. I tried to hide my wet face, but Grandma Lollie noticed right away.

She motioned for me to sit on her bed. She took my hand and examined it. She saw that there was no bite. She looked relieved.

I wiped my nose with my sleeve. "Can I tell you something?" I asked her. She nodded and smiled. I told her all about the test and my mom. I told her about my new school. I told her about my dad and Las Vegas. I told her that my mom probably wouldn't let me go now.

Lollie squeezed my hand. She wrote on her white board, "Explain it to your mom the way you explained it to me. She'll understand." Maybe she was right. Lollie erased the board and wrote, "Take the day off!" But I didn't want to - I wanted to delay seeing my mom as long as possible.

Augustus and I went outside. We walked quickly against the wind. My heart was pounding. The wind blew into my face. My eyes got teary again, maybe from the wind or maybe because I was crying some more.

As we turned the corner, I glanced at Augustus. He looked full of energy. I knew he could keep up. I broke into a run. Augustus followed immediately. I ran as hard and fast as I could. My sneakers slapped against the sidewalk. My black scarf streamed out behind me. We ran and ran. My limbs were moving wildly. Augustus ran neatly, legs folding and unfolding perfectly, as if he were a machine. My lungs were screaming from the cold, but we kept going.

We ran all the way to Jones Park where I used to play when I was a kid. Then I stopped, and leaned on a bench, and tried to catch my breath. Augustus was panting but his eyes were shining. I sat on the bench, and he hopped up next to me. I found a little hunk of of Slim Jim in my coat pocket. He gobbled it up. Then he leaned his little body against me. I could feel his breathing become more regular. I was still gasping for air.

Walks with Augustus

14

I hung around at Lollie's as long as I could. When I finally got home it was dark outside. My mom was sitting at the kitchen table with a cup of tea. There was just one light on in the apartment.

"Hi," I said.

"Hi," she said, her voice tense. I decided to take Grandma Lollie's advice. I told my mom everything. When

I finished, I searched for the same kind look that Lollie had given me. I didn't find it.

"Sofia, you know this is completely unacceptable," she said. I wished she were yelling. It was worse when she was too mad to yell.

"I don't know what to do. I thought the structure of doing this thing for Lollie would be enough. But you've gotten worse."

"I haven't gotten worse! It was one time-" I began.

"Enough," she said sternly. "This is serious. I've talked it over with your dad, and we agree that you shouldn't visit Vegas over break. If you want such an expensive privilege, you have to earn it. It's a distraction from your school work, anyway."

In a way I had expected this, but I still couldn't believe it. I had been looking forward to Vegas ever since Dad left. How could she keep me from my dad?

"You can't do that!" I yelled. "Dad won't let you!" I pulled out my phone to call him.

"He's already agreed," she said.

"Yeah, right," I growled. I stormed into my bedroom and slammed the door. I dialed my dad. He would be prepping for the dinner service but I had to talk to him. He answered on the fourth ring.

"Hi sweetie," he said.

"Dad, tell her she can't make me stay here!" I cried. "It was just one time, I'm never doing it again. I promise."

His voice was much gentler than my mom's. "This is what we agreed is best, Sofia. You need to improve your school work."

"Dad!" I started sobbing. He was the one who normally took my side. He was the one who said it was okay if I wasn't great at school. I could still be great at other things.

"I'm sorry, honey," he said. He sounded sad. "It's not permanent. I'll see you next week for Thanksgiving. You can come for another break once you improve your work."

"Okay," I said, my voice thick with tears. My eyes burned and my head was throbbing. I lay in bed for a while staring at the ceiling. My stomach started growling, so I crept into the kitchen. My mom was gone. I made a frozen pizza. I ate it at the table, with one light on, by myself.

15

I left for school the next morning without talking to my mom. I didn't feel like talking to anyone at school either. When the bell rang for dismissal, I pushed out the doors with the rest of the kids. I walked down the sidewalk with my head down. Then, I heard someone call my name.

"Sofia! Over here!"

It was Asha, waving from the window of her mom's blue Toyota.

"Come shopping with us!" Natalie cried, popping her head out of the other window. I went over to the car.

"I cant, I have to walk Augustus," I said, feeling glum.

"Come on, please?" Natalie pleaded. "You can miss one day."

Then I remembered what Lollie had said about giving me a day off. She said it was fine yesterday, so why not today? I really wanted to go with them.

Just then, Omar went by on his crutches. "Hey, he called to me with a smile. See you at home?"

"Tell Mikhail I can't come today," I replied. I opened the door and hopped in.

"Okay," Omar said, looking a little confused. We sped off towards the mall.

"Who was that?" asked Natalie, nudging me.

Asha chimed in, "He was cute."

"He's just a guy. He lives in Lollie's building," I said. I tried to sound casual.

"He likes you," Natalie announced.

I rolled my eyes. "Whatever," I said. I turned to look out the window, hiding a smile.

16

Shopping for things for other people is pretty boring. I watched them try on dress after dress for the Winter Dance. But it was nice to hang out with Asha and Natalie like I used to. A few times I had a little pang of guilt. I should be at Lollie's. I argued with myself in my head. You deserve a break, I would say. Then I would answer myself, But Lollie and Augustus need you. I tried to smoosh those feelings down and have fun.

After five or six stores, Asha finally found a dress. It was turquoise and sparkly. It looked great on her. Natalie went home empty-handed.

I got home before my mom. I made myself chocolate milk and a peanut butter and banana sandwich.

My dad called that sandwich The Elvis. He used to make it for me as a treat when I was little.

I took everything into my room and closed the door. I put my headphones on and read magazines all night. I picked a bunch of dresses that I would wear if I were going to a dance. If I were, would I ask Omar?

I didn't even take out my homework, but I didn't care. I needed a break, I said to myself again. I re-painted my nails and tried on makeup. I only came out of my room to brush my teeth. I fell asleep before my mom came home.

17

I woke up the next morning before my alarm. I felt panicked but I didn't know why. Then I remembered: I hadn't done any of my homework. I switched on the desk lamp and pulled out my binders.

I quickly filled out my Spanish worksheet. Then I looked up my vocabulary words. I could do my reading on the bus. The only thing left was algebra. I groaned quietly and pulled out my textbook. I tried the first problem. The numbers and letters swirled together on the page like they always did.

I couldn't do it. It was too hard. I was bad at math. It was stupid for me to even waste my time trying. I scratched some numbers on to the page to make it look like I did the homework. The teacher didn't collect it to check. She just walked around the room to look. I hoped that would be enough.

Even though I'd woken up early I was running late. The bus I got on was crowded and made every stop. It was good, because I had more time to catch up on my reading for English and history. But it made me even later. When I finally got off, I sprinted from the bus stop to school. I charged through the double doors. I almost crashed into someone. It turned out to be Omar.

"Sofia! Are you okay?" he asked.

"Yeah, why?" I said. My eye was on the clock in the hallway. One minute until the bell.

"You left in a rush after school. I thought something was wrong." Omar had circles under his eyes. His voice was a little scratchy.

"Why would something be wrong?" I said. Thirty seconds till the bell.

He shrugged. His normal energy was gone. "I don't know. Did your mom tell you what happened?"

The warning bell rang. It meant there were 15 seconds to get to homeroom.

"I haven't talked to her," I said. "Anyway, I'm late. Tell me at Lollie's," I called over my should as I jogged toward homeroom.

I made it just in time.

18

When I got to Lollie's that afternoon, something wasn't right. The curtains were drawn. Normally they were open, with Lollie in the middle watching the sidewalk. I got a bad feeling that I couldn't explain. I hurried up the stairs and rang the buzzer. There was no answer. I thought to call Mikhail but realized I didn't have his number. I rang the buzzer a few more times and sat on the stoop to wait.

After a few minutes, an old maroon colored sedan pulled up and parked. It was Omar, Leila, and their mom. He got out of the car, and I realized his crutches were gone.

"Hey, your cast is off! Nice," I said.

"Thanks. Still got a brace though," he said. I expected him to be more excited.

"Hi Sofia," said Nadia. "I didn't think you'd still be coming, but it's a good idea. Augustus still needs his walk."

"What do you mean?" I said.

"We had him in our apartment last night, but he snapped at Leila and now she cries whenever she sees him," she went on.

Omar saw the confused look on my face. "She doesn't know yet, Mom."

"Oh, honey," she said. "I'll let Omar tell you then," she said, shaking her head. She headed up the stairs with Leila.

I turned to Omar. "What's going on?" I demanded.

"Let's talk about it inside," was all he said. Omar got up the stairs with remarkable speed. It was almost like he'd never broken his leg.

"What happened?" I asked again. Omar undid the deadbolt to Lollie's apartment and stepped inside. He motioned me in. It was dark. No one was there. Then I saw the white outline of Augustus. He was curled up on Lollie's bed by the window. "Where is she?" I asked.

Omar flipped on a light. "She had another stroke last night," he began. "They had to take her to the hospital. She's there now.

I was quiet for a minute. I went and sat with Augustus.He looked up at me with his deep brown eyes. They were perfect circles. I'd never noticed that before. He let me scratch behind his ears.

"She'll be okay, right?" I asked Omar. "She'll be home soon?"

"They aren't sure," Omar said. "Mikhail said it doesn't look good."

I felt my face get hot. A hard lump formed in my throat. I pushed back tears.

"Mikhail's been staying at the hospital, driving the nurses there crazy," he said with a soft laugh. "We're going to visit her tomorrow, my mom and me. You should come. She's not awake, but Mikhail said it's good to talk to her," he said. I nodded slowly.

I looked around the apartment. It had seemed so alive just two days ago. Lollie's favorite records were always playing.

She would play cards or read when she wasn't watching her city out the window. Mikhail was always busy, tidying or cooking or helping Lollie. Augustus was dancing around, or snoring, or doing whatever what he liked to do.

Now it was too quiet. Everything seemed lifeless. I took a deep breath. "I should walk him, I guess," I said.

"Good idea," said Omar.

"Where's he going tonight?" I asked.

"He's staying here for tonight. After that I don't know. Lollie's niece is allergic. My mom's trying to find another family member who will take him in."

I nodded. I clipped the brown leash on the little white dog.

Augustus and I stepped out into the cold together.

19

As we walked, Augustus seemed focused. For once he ignored all the other dogs and people. He kept his head up and pushed forward. We walked our usual 45 minute route in 30 minutes. He barely stopped to sniff.

When we got back to the apartment he charged in and looked around. He looked in every room. He sniffed all the doorways carefully. When he was sure no one was there, he hopped back up on the hospital bed. He curled up and breathed a sad, deep sigh.

I poured some kibble in his dish, but he wasn't interested. I checked to make sure he could use his doggy door to the backyard. I changed his water. He didn't seem to noticed me puttering around the apartment.

I looked at the bookcase in the living room. It was covered in framed photos. There were color photos of Lollie's family. Then there was a black and white one of Lollie at her wedding. She wore a white suit, and her husband had on a military uniform. I wasn't sure when he died, but I had never met him.

Another picture showed Lollie on a stage, in front of a microphone. She was young. Her hair was long and blond and her face smiling. She wore a beautiful satin gown. On the white border of the picture, someone had written "1946."

Then I looked at her books. They were biographies of singers from Billie Holiday to Sarah Bernhardt. There were George Gershwin songbooks.

I guess I was feeling nosy. I opened what I thought had been the coat closet. I realized it held her record collection. There were hundreds of them. They were organized alphabetically. I carefully slid a few out. There was opera and jazz. There was Janis Joplin and Whitney Houston. A collection full of strong voices.

For some reason, I hadn't realized that Lollie was a singer. How had I missed it? I thought about what it meant for her to lose her voice. I understood why Mikhail had made it his mission to help her get it back. I wanted to help, too. I would do whatever I could. I put the records back as I found them.

Before I left, I checked on Augustus one more time. I scratched behind his ears cautiously. I was worried he might bite me, but he just looked up at me for a second, and then laid his head back down.

"She'll be home soon," I said. I left a light on for him, and slipped outside.

20

By the time I got home it was dinnertime. My mom was working late again. I didn't feel like cooking anything. I made a giant bowl of cereal. Then I looked through my mom's dusty CD collection. I put on an Ella Fitzgerald album. It didn't sound the same as at Lollie's. Maybe it was true that CDs didn't sound as good as records. But still it was nice to hear Ella's voice, which was smooth and strong. I ate my cereal and did my homework at the kitchen table, just like at Lollie's.

I was finishing up my reading when I heard the lock squeak open. It was nearly 9:30. I knew my mom had had a busy day. I knew she was probably still mad at me, too. I didn't want to fight with her tonight.

When she came in, she had a worried look on her face. She put her things down and took off her coat. Her eyes were red.

"What's wrong?" I asked.

She sat down next to me. "I just talked to Mikhail. He was calling with news about Lollie."

"I know, she had another stroke. We're going to go see her tomorrow," I said.

"No, honey," she said, taking my hand. "He called to say she passed away tonight."

Suddenly everything seemed very quiet. The music faded to nothing. All I could hear was my own heartbeat. My mom was still talking. But I didn't hear a word of it. I sat very still for what felt like a long time.

"I need to go to bed," I heard myself say.

"Okay honey," she said. She gave me a big hug.

I went to my room and put on my headphones. I picked out my loudest, fastest music. I cranked the volume so high I thought my eardrums would burst. I climbed into bed with all my clothes on. I pulled the covers up over my head. I let the music drown out everything else. I thought I would cry. I wanted to cry. But my eyes felt as dry as a desert.

21

I woke up in the middle of the night. Everything was dark and quiet. My dream had left a song in my head. "Someone to Watch Over Me," by Ella Fitzgerald. I felt sad but I couldn't remember why. Then it came back to me: Lollie had died.

Finally the tears came. The lump that had been in my throat finally burst. I sobbed into my pillow.

She wasn't the first person I knew to have died. My grandparents died when I was little. But they lived far away and I didn't see them much.

I felt empty and sad. And guilty, too. I hadn't seen her on her last day. I skipped out to go shopping. I knew that me being there wouldn't have changed anything. But still. I skipped walking Augustus to hang out with my friends.

I thought of Augustus. He was by himself in the apartment. Was he scared? Did he know somehow that she wasn't coming back? Was he lonely? I pictured him as I'd seen him that afternoon: curled up and quiet on her bed. Waiting. Alone. I couldn't leave him there.

Without thinking much, I hopped out of bed. The clock said 1:30 am. I blew my nose and grabbed my shoes and bag. I tip-toed out of my room.

I slipped out the door and locked it softly. I put on my shoes in the hallway. I was halfway down the stairs when I realized I forgot my coat. But I was afraid I'd wake my mom if I went back for it. The air outside hit me like a kick in the guts. But somehow it felt good, too. It dried up my tears as I walked to the bus stop. For once, the bus came quickly. It was nearly empty. I started at my reflection in the window and tried to rub the streaks of eyeliner off my face.

In no time I was standing in front of Lollie's building. Then I realized the problem with my plan. I didn't have keys to the front door. It was almost two in the morning, so I couldn't ring any of the buzzers. I didn't have anyone's number. And it didn't matter, because I had forgotten my phone.

I rattled the door a little just to see if would open. It didn't. I found a paperclip in my bag and tried to pick the lock like in the movies. It wouldn't budge. Frustrated, I even kicked the door. I thought of Lollie. I thought of Augustus. I just needed to get him. The hot tears started flowing again. "Why won't you just open?" I whisper-sobbed at the door.

Suddenly, the light went on in the hallway. Omar and his mom were squinting at me. When Nadia recognized me, she sighed. She looked kind of mad. Omar opened the door and I squeezed inside.

"What are you doing? We thought you were a burglar!" she whispered.

Because I had been crying, my words came out funny. "I'm here. For Augustus," I said. "He shouldn't be alone!" I started crying again. Her face softened.

"It's okay," she said. "Omar will let you in. Take all the time you need."

If it were a normal day, I'd be embarrassed to cry in front of Omar. But this was not a normal day. For one thing, it was two in the morning.

He opened the door to the apartment. Augustus was right inside, waiting. I flipped on the light and sat down to pet him. He climbed into my lap. He rested his head on my hand and sighed.

"Hey, he finally likes you," Omar said with a smile. He sat down on the floor with us.

"I'm taking him home. He'll stay with me, at least until things are figured out," I said.

"That sounds good. But we could have decided that tomorrow, you know," he said.

I smiled. "No, I couldn't let him be alone."

"Does your mom know you're here?" asked Omar.

I winced. "No, she was sleeping. She doesn't really like dogs either. She probably would have said no," I replied.

He laughed. "So maybe this was a good plan."

"Hope so," I said. I gently lifted Augustus off my lap. I got up and gathered up his toys, his food, and his dog bowl, and stuffed them in my bag. I got his leash.

As Omar was locking up the apartment, his mom tiptoed down the stairs and handed me a sweatshirt. "How are you getting home?"

"I guess I'll walk. I can't take him on the bus," I said.

"By yourself? No way," she said. "I'm calling your mom."

I panicked. "No, please! She...she doesn't know I'm here. She's sleeping," I said.

"Well, I'm not letting you walk home by yourself in the middle of the night. Omar, you go with her," she said.

"No, I'm okay," I said. I didn't want to bother them more than I already had.

"No, she's right," Omar said. "Let me just get my coat."

22

Augustus and I waited out front for Omar. I was warmer in the sweatshirt, but still chilly. Augustus sniffed around at the tree outside. I looked up into the cloudy sky.

Omar came down the steps and handed me a hat and gloves. "Ready?" he asked. I nodded, and we began quickly walking towards my house. It was normally about a thirty-minute walk. We spent most of it in silence. The only sounds were the wind in the bare tree branches and my sniffling.

"She was a singer, you know," I said suddenly.

"Lollie?" he asked.

"Yeah. At least, I think so."

"You're right. She did it professionally. She was even a back up singer on some famous songs. She was still teaching voice students until a few years ago," he said.

"How do you know so much about her?" I asked.

"I grew up in that building. She was like family," he said. "She was going to turn 90 this year. We were planning to have a big party."

I felt bad all over again. Here I was crying my eyes out, and I didn't even ask how he was doing. Without thinking about it, I grabbed his hand and gave it a squeeze. He squeezed back. "I'm sorry," I said. "I didn't know how close you were to her."

"She was like family to a lot of people. She didn't have kids, so she treated everyone like they were hers."

As we passed under the streetlight I realized that snow had begun to fall. Soon a light layer dusted the three of us. Augustus shook off the snow. His tags jingled like bells.

We rounded the corner onto my street. I could see that a light was on in the apartment. My mom was up. She had to know I wasn't there. This wasn't going to be fun.

"It's cool that you came to get Augustus," Omar said. "Honestly I don't think anyone else was ready to take him. He's not the nicest dog."

"I think he's good at heart," I said. "People just don't understand him."

We arrived in front of my house. Omar and I faced each other.

"You gonna be okay?" Omar asked.

"I guess. How about you?" I said.

"I guess."

I got my keys out. "I should go in," I said. But I didn't move. Omar smiled a little half smile. I looked at the ground, feeling embarrassed for some reason. I looked up again and smiled, too. He leaned toward me and gave me a soft, quick kiss.

I was so stunned, I didn't say anything. He gave Augustus a pet, and then told me goodnight. He jogged off toward the bus stop, waving to me as he went. He was still a little wobbly when he ran on the bad leg. He left jagged footprints in the new snow.

23

I stood on the sidewalk for a minute, trying to process what just happened. The cold wind quickly brought me back to reality. I coaxed Augustus up the snowy steps and wondered how I would explain this to my mom.

As I turned the key and opened the door, I heard her talking on the phone. "Oh, thank God, that's her. I'll call you back," she said. I peeked my head in the door and looked at my mom. Her face was puffy and red. "Sofia

Alvarez, if you ever leave this house in the middle of the night again..." Just then, Augustus nosed the door all the way open and trotted in. "What is that?" my mom asked.

"That's Augustus," I said simply. "He was alone. He needs someone to take care of him. I couldn't leave him there. Yell at me if you want."

She looked shocked. For the first time probably in her whole life, she was speechless. She looked at me, then at him, and then at me again.

I took Augustus to my room. I got changed into my warmest pajamas. I made a dog bed for him out of some towels, but he didn't like it. He scratched at the side of my bed and whined. "You want to sleep with me?" I asked him. "Okay, but no biting me during the night," I said as I lifted him onto the bed. I climbed in and got under the covers.

There was a knock at the door, and my mom came in. She was holding two steaming mugs. "I made us some chamomile tea. Though I probably won't be able to get back to sleep. You really scared me," she said.

"Sorry," I said. "I thought you'd say no. And anyway I couldn't let him spend the night alone. I kind of freaked out," I admitted. The grouchy dog rolled over so that he was leaning hard against my legs. He sighed deeply.

"I should probably punish you," she began. "You did a good thing, even if you went about it in the wrong way. Next time try not to give me a heart attack."

"Okay," I said. I took a sip of tea. She made it just the way I liked it, with the perfect amount of honey. She sat down on the bed. "I know things haven't been great between us lately. It's been a tough year for both of us. But you know I love you more than anything right?"

I did know it. I knew it deep down. But sometimes I didn't always feel it, I guess.

"I know," I said. "I love you, too." She gave me a hug. She reached down to pet Augustus. He growled at her.

"Nice dog," she said, rolling her eyes.

"Yeah," I said. "We get each other."

24

Grandma Lollie's funeral was the following Sunday. My dad came early for Thanksgiving so he could go to the service with us. The three of us squeezed into the packed church. It was full of her family and friends. Lollie had made a difference to so many people.

Afterwards, we went back to her apartment. The day before, my dad and I helped Omar's mom cook lots of things for the lunch after the funeral. Loads of people came to the house. They told stories about Lollie. Omar put on some of her favorite records. It was sad, but nice.

I brought Augustus to the reception. He stuck to me like glue. He was crabby around crowds, but I thought he should be there. He was Lollie's family, too.

He and I sat on the floor in the hall, listening to everyone in the living room. I said it was because Augustus didn't like strangers. But I also felt like being by myself. I let the voices and music wash over me. Lollie would have liked this, I thought. All those voices filling up her house.

I was so focused on the voices that I didn't hear my dad's step until he was right next to me. He had a plate with some of the food he'd made. Lollie's family had come from Poland, so he made Polish dumplings, called pierogi, for the reception. They were stuffed with potatoes and cheese and fried with onions. He sat down on the floor next to me, and we dug into the plate together. I'd forgotten how much I loved just having a meal with him.

I gave Augustus half a pierogi. He gobbled it down.

"This has been some year, huh?" my dad said between bites. I grunted in reply. "I know you've had a tough few months," he said. I shrugged. I didn't really want to talk about it. "Anyway, I was talking to Nadia. Did you know she used to be a math teacher?" my dad said. I shook my head no. "Well, we were talking about you, and you know she thinks you're really great, right? She said she wants to help you with your algebra. You can come by after school and do homework with her."

"Okay," I said. It didn't sound exactly thrilling, but it was nice of her. Plus, I'd get to see Omar.

"Okay, you'll do it?" he said.

"Yeah, I guess. Why?"

"Well, I got mom to agree that if you got some tutoring, she'd let you come visit over break after all," he said.

"No way!" I gasped.

"Yup. And there's a spot for you to learn in the kitchen, if you want it," he added.

"Of course I want it!" I said. I laughed, just out of happiness. I looked at the scruffy white dog next to me. "Can Augustus come too?"

"Of course!" he said. Then he wrapped me in a big hug.

Just then the buzzer rang. Natalie and Asha walked in. "We're really sorry about Grandma Lollie," Asha said.

"We wanted to see if you wanted to go to the movies or something," said Natalie. "Or we can hang out here if you want to stay."

"Sofia, you should go with them," said my dad. "We'll finish up here, and bring Augustus home."

I looked down at my new little friend. He looked up at me and blinked. "Okay," I said. "But I should walk him first."

"Good idea," my dad said. "Let's all get a little fresh air."

The day was unseasonably warm. The sun shone down and warmed my back as we hopped down the steps. Asha and Natalie came out, and then my dad, my mom, and Omar, too.

We walked the length of the block without speaking.

We listened to the birds chirping like crazy. They were happy it was a warm day, I guess. I thought about the people I was walking with. I'd felt so alone the last few months. But here we all were, walking with a little white dog. They were all different. None of them were exactly like me, but that was okay. That was great, actually.

A squirrel skittered across our path and Augustus barked at it. A silver Jeep drove by, blasting reggae through the open windows. A group of little girls on bikes rode down the street, ringing their bells. And I realized the air was filled with music.

Walks with Augustus

About The Author

L. V. Halo is a writer living in Jersey City, NJ. Growing up, some of her best friends were the people (and animals) she found in books. The Story Shares contest, and the way that a relationship with reading can sometimes be fraught, inspired Halo to write a story of unlikely friendship. She recently earned a Master's degree in English and creative writing from Fordham University, and is currently at work on a middle-grade historical novel. This is her first published work of fiction.

Walks with Augustus

About The Publisher

Story Shares is a nonprofit focused on supporting the millions of teens and adults who struggle with reading by creating a new shelf in the library specifically for them. The ever-growing collection features content that is compelling and culturally relevant for teens and adults, yet still readable at a range of lower reading levels.

Story Shares generates content by engaging deeply with writers, bringing together a community to create this new kind of book. With more intriguing and approachable stories to choose from, the teens and adults who have fallen behind are improving their skills and beginning to discover the joy of reading. For more information, visit storyshares.org.

Easy to Read. Hard to Put Down.

Made in the USA
Middletown, DE
20 January 2023

22139890R00071